Idunn's Rescue

Loki lured Idunn out of Ásgard into a certain wood, saying that he had found such apples as would seem to her of great virtue, and prayed that she would have her apples with her and compare them with these.

Snorri Sturluson, Skáldskaparmál, p. 91

"Where is Idunn?!"

The cry resonated throughout Ásgard, for the goddess of youth, renewal and vitality had not been seen in the realm of the Æsir for some time. Her absence was becoming more and more conspicuous with the passing of the days, since the golden apples she grew in her garden were the food which helped keep the gods youthful and vigorous. Not partaking of Idunn's apples was making the Æsir feel weaker and some, particularly the goddesses, look noticeably older.

Finally, Odin assembled all the denizens of Valhalla in the vast greeting hall of the palace and asked them, one by one, when they had last seen Idunn. Most of those questioned could give only vague answers, or none at all.

Idunn's younger sister Nanna, however, had a specific recollection: "I do not remember the exact date, for it has been some time, but she left early one morning from Valhalla's gate carrying her ash-wood apple box."

"Was she alone?"

"Yes and no," replied Nanna. "Loki was following her, a few steps behind."

There was a collective intake of breath. Odin asked sharply: "Is this true, Loki?"

Loki hesitated for a moment. Dissembling came to him as naturally as breathing, but lying to Odin was dangerous and often futile, for the greatest of the gods could find the truth on any matter by traveling to the well at the world's tree Yggdrasil and talking to the embalmed head of Mimir, the dead sage who knows all that is. "I may have gone out at the same time as Idunn, but not necessarily gone *with* her . . ."

Odin was familiar with his blood brother's duplicity, and asked in a commanding tone: "Well, did you in fact go out with Idunn on the occasion reported by Nanna?"

Loki realized he would not be able to get away with deceit this time. "Yes, I did," he replied sheepishly.

"So, where did the two of you go?"

"To the big forest at the eastern edge of the Plain of Idavöll, just before the mountains."

"For what purpose did you go to that forest?"

"I had told Idunn that in my travels through the forest I had discovered a hidden grove of ancient apple trees, and having plucked an apple from one of those trees I had discerned that it was at least as good, and perhaps tastier, than the apples she grows and carries in her magic box. She came with me to put my comparison to the test."

"And what happened in the forest? Did she try the apples from the hidden grove?"

Loki shook his head. "No. Thiazi, one of the frost giants we met in our travels to Jötunheim, was sitting atop a tree, disguised as an eagle. All of a sudden, he glided down, seized Idunn, and flew away with her."

There was a long pause. Odin's next question was more of an accusation: "And was it just a coincidence that you led Idunn to the forest while Thiazi was there, lying in wait?"

Loki was about to try and spin a lie, but read danger in Odin's rigid face. "No, brother. Thiazi beat me in a game of dice and made me swear an oath that I would deliver Idunn to him, for he was eager to taste her golden apples and savor the most precious one, Idunn herself."

A roar of indignation shook the thick walls of Valhalla. With barely contained rage, Odin rendered judgment on his blood brother: "You shall recover Idunn from captivity and bring her back to Ásgard, unharmed. And you must do it very soon because I swear by Gungnir that otherwise I shall run your miserable body through with my spear and plant you on the ground for the crows to feast on!"

Loki found himself surrounded by angry gods who were only held back from assaulting him by Odin's protection. He realized that swift action was required to save his skin.

He dared not arrive in Jötunheim and confront the formidable giant Thiazi directly, and in any case, stealth was his preferred mode of operation. He would conceal his presence and wait for the right opportunity to strike. He decided to render himself unnoticed by borrowing, as he had done on other occasions, Freyja's falcon-feather mantle, which allowed him to travel to the land of the giants in the form of a bird. Thus, under cover of darkness, Loki flew to Jötunheim and took a position on a tree near Thiazi's fortress.

He waited three days before an opportunity presented itself. On the fourth day he saw Thiazi assume the form of a gigantic eagle. The giant flew from his domain, leaving the prisoner unattended. Loki turned himself into a titmouse so he could squeeze through the bars of the room in which Idunn was imprisoned. Entering, he spoke to her:

"It is I, Loki, come to rescue you!"

Idunn was not pleased to see him. "Why should I put my trust in you, after the way you lied and delivered me to this monster?"

Loki replied, using the most contrite tones in his repertory: "I will forever rue the day that necessity forced me to betray you. But this is not the time for recriminations. Thiazi has gone away, but could return any moment. Come now with me, or you may have to remain his guest forever!"

Idunn sighed and approached the titmouse, which turned back into a falcon and enveloped the goddess between the folds of the mantle. Instantly, she became an orange and yellow goldcrest. Holding the tiny bird delicately on his beak, Loki flew out of the prison and darted away to freedom, still in falcon form.

As they were crossing back into Ásgard, Loki felt a disturbance in the air. Turning around, he saw a giant eagle approaching them. Redoubling his efforts, he sent an urgent non-verbal call to the gods below: "HELP!"

In a matter of minutes, the gods gathered outside Valhalla to watch with awe as two birds approached. A smaller falcon came on ahead, a large eagle chasing after. The eagle was gaining on its prey, opening and closing its talons in anticipation of tearing it apart. But Odin commanded urgently: "Thor, throw your hammer!"

Without hesitation, Thor grasped Mjölnir, his magical hammer, twirled it once above his head and released it heavenward. As directed by Thor's will, the hammer flew at the eagle, striking its chest with a loud bang that could be heard clearly by those assembled below.

Thiazi, regaining his gigantic shape, plunged to the ground and crashed a few feet away from Valhalla's gate, leaving a crater that would continue to release fulsome vapors for many seasons afterward.

Idunn's rescue was thus successfully accomplished, but that was not the end of the matter. Skadi, Thiazi's daughter, was aggrieved at the unjust slaying of her father. She assembled an army of frost giants and prepared to march across the rainbow bridge Bifröst and lay waste to Ásgard.

Odin, riding his eight-legged steed Sleipnir, met the giants at the foot of the bridge. "Ho, Skadi, this is not the day for war to break between our races. Ragnarøkkr is, hopefully, a long time into the future! Can we please hold peaceful discourse to address your grievances?"

Skadi, who was less ferocious than her father, agreed to hold talks. Along with a delegation of giants she was invited to Valhalla under a flag of truce. They joined Odin and the Æsir in a long discussion, culminating in a banquet where roasted meats and strong ale were freely consumed. Odin agreed to pay wergild for Thiazi's death. In addition to the compensation in gold, he cast the giant's eyes into the heavens to become new stars.

Skadi was almost satisfied, but set another condition: "The guilty one, the rascal who caused my father's demise, needs to be punished."

Odin would not consent to punishing one of his peers, but agreed that Loki needed to be chastised. "How about public shaming?" he suggested.

Skadi frowned, but bowed her head in acquiescence.

That is how it came to pass that on Haustblot, the fall equinox, Valhalla held a large celebration to which a delegation of giants from Jötunheim were invited. Skadi sat as guest of honor next to Odin. She, and the other attendees, waited in silent expectation as a naked Loki and a black she-goat were led into the hall. Horns sounded, drums beat, and all guests broke down into laughter as Loki attempted to copulate with the goat. Having to withstand the kicks and bites of the displeased beast, he complained loudly, meanwhile secretly enjoying the grotesque performance.

Thor's Fear

A GIGANTIC KETTLE BRIMMING WITH ALE was brought again and again to the long tables and dispensed to the gods and elves attending the sea god Ægir's feast. Fueled by the liquor, the guests were drinking convivially and sharing each other's company in good cheer. Outside the hall, however, stood an uninvited deity: Loki, the god of mischief and discord.

Loki stopped one of Ægir's serving men and questioned him: "Eldir, what are they saying inside about me while sipping their ale?"

"Nothing. They only talk about their weapons and

their might in war; nobody mentions you at all."

"I shall change that. They must not forget me. I will go in and bring some venom to mix with the ale, and spice up the party that way."

"Beware, for the gods would likely punish you for such an evil deed," warned the serving man.

"Your words bring joy to my heart. Watch me!" Loki shoved the servant aside and strode into the hall, where he was met by an immediate wall of silence.

"Will you give me mead to quench my thirst?" he demanded.

Nobody answered, and Loki insisted: "Come on! Either offer me drink and a seat at your table, or have the ill grace to send me away!"

The gods were still reluctant to seat Loki, but at last he invoked his blood kinship with Odin, who directed that Loki be given a seat and ale to drink. No sooner had he been seated than did Loki start to insult, one by one, each of the gods and goddesses in attendance, casting aspersions on the gods' courage and the goddesses' chastity and faithfulness.

But Loki's tirade was soon interrupted by the arrival of

the god Thor, coming home from a trip abroad. Thor was Odin's son and a powerful deity himself. He was associated with lightning, thunder, and fertility. Thor wielded Mjölnir, a magical hammer that allowed him to strike without fail, as heavily as he liked, whatever the target, and never flew so far that it would not find its way back to his hand.

Thor chided Loki for his abuse of the other gods:

"Loki, cease your ill-mannered words, seeking to demean your betters, or Mjölnir shall close thy mouth; I shall hurl you up and out into Jötunheim, where neither gods nor me shall see thee e'er again."

At the mention of Jötunheim, the realm of the frost giants, Loki quickly retorted: "You should make no mention of Jötunheim, lest you be asked how you fared there. For I was with you and witnessed how you cowered and forgot yourself."

Loki did not mention that in Jötunheim they had come to the domain of the sorcerer Skrymir, who had subjected Thor and his companions to enchantments destined to frighten the travelers and cause them to flee back to the world of the Æsir.

Thor refused to engage Loki in an argument. Instead, he repeated in a dangerous tone:

"Loki, cease your ill-mannered speech, or the mighty hammer Mjölnir shall close thy mouth; with it, I shall send you to hell, and down to the gate of death."

This new threat, accompanied by Thor's start in his direction, caused Loki to rise: "Before you alone I yield, for you fight well, I suppose." Loki then fled the hall precipitously.

Later, after leaving Ægir's feast, Thor and his wife Sif mounted their goat-driven chariot and returned to Bilskirnir, their hall in the heart of Ásgard. Thor's mood always lightened when he returned to his prized palace, a building said to be the largest ever erected. Not this time, however. He was still sullen when Sif led him to their chamber, caressed him, and sought to entice him into making love. Finding him unresponsive, Sif asked: "Husband, what dark cloud hovers over your spirit? It is not like you to fail to rise to the allure of the flesh."

Thor sighed and responded: "My encounter with that rascal Loki has left me in no mood for love."

Sif laughed. "It makes little sense for you to pay attention to anything that deceiving scoundrel says. Do you remember how once he stole my hair and you forced him, under threat of death, to go down to Svartálfheim, find the dark elves' master craftsmen, and have them construct a new head of hair for me? Loki is but a rat, deathly afraid of you. You should ignore him."

"It was not what Loki said, but the memories his speech brought back," replied Thor. "In Skrymir's evil domain, the sorcerer put me through three trials. I had to drink from a horn whose contents I could never finish (for, in reality, I was drinking from the ocean); then I was made, and was barely able, to lift a large cat (in reality, it was the World Serpent Jörmungandr, the supreme monster I am fated to engage in the final battle of Ragnarøkkr); and finally, I had to wrestle with a frail-looking old woman, who nonetheless defeated me and made me drop one knee to the ground—as it turned out, it was Old Age I fought, an invincible opponent."

"But those were just enchantments, and their outcome should not have troubled you."

"They did not, in themselves. I was never going to be able to drink away an entire ocean, though as it turned out I caused its level to drop noticeably. Nor could I overpower Jörmungandr, for we are fated to have a decisive encounter much later, at the end of time. However, when Skrymir revealed that the crone who forced me to bend my knee was *old age*, I became quite disturbed. Unlike humans, I thought that, thanks to Idunn's apples, we gods were immune from the pains and indignities of growing old. I accept the inevitability of perishing at Ragnarøkkr, but who knows how much farther into the future that accursed day will be? What if I have gotten old and infirm, my limbs weakened and pained by age and disease, long before the end arrives? I can accept dying like a hero, but I fear limping through season after season like a helpless human."

Sif laughed again. "I thought manly heroes like yourself were made of sterner stuff. We females must endure the disappointment of losing our looks, the pains of childbirth, the anxiety over the possible loss of our consorts in battle. Cast your fears aside, for you males have it easy. When old age comes, you will most likely be facing opponents who are as diminished as you are. Yours is the luckier sex, so you should enjoy your privileges until the end of days! And, speaking of enjoyment, let us pleasure each other and forget the distant future!"

Thor's misgivings were not allayed, yet he forced himself to cast a rueful smile. "Females are not only the stronger sex, but also the wiser one," he conceded, and kissed her.

Freyja's Necklace

The avarice of dwarves and the arrogance of elves are well known.
But so are the temptations of humans.
Neha Teena, The Keeper of Rhymes

IT WAS THE FOURTH NIGHT OF JUL, the twelve-day festival in which gods and men celebrated the Midwinter Solstice with feasts and contests that ran long into the early hours of the morning. Freyja, Odin's consort and the goddess of love and beauty, was traveling back to her own palace after an evening of celebration at Valhalla. She rode on her chariot, drawn by two cats.

Suddenly the weather turned stormy: heavy snow began to fall and a strong wind gusted from the north, becoming a true blizzard. Freyja, as a goddess, was impervious to the weather, but the cats had difficulty finding their way on the road and soon the chariot came to a halt.

They had been stranded for some time when Freyja's

keen vision spotted a glow ahead and to their right. She drove the cats in that direction, and they came upon the source of illumination. There was a deep cave on a hillside by the road, with bright light emanating from its opening. Freyja hopped out of the chariot and strode to the entrance of the cave. As she approached, her ears filled with the discordant clanging of metal striking metal.

Descending into the cave, Freyja found herself in a smithy where four dark elves were working on a golden necklace. The necklace was exquisite, gleaming as though it were the morning sun. It held a heavy pendant in the form of a standing woman surrounded by seven precious stones in alternating hues of forest green, amber, and dark red.

Freyja glanced at the piece of jewelry and marveled aloud: "That is beautiful!"

The leader of the dark elves, who called himself Dvalinn, replied graciously: "This necklace is called Brísingamen and is pretty fair, but not as beautiful as you, my Lady."

Freyja was used to the acclamation of gods and the worship of humans, so she did not assign much value to a compliment from a lowly svartálfr. She said: "I am the spouse of all-powerful Odin. I would like to purchase Brísingamen. Name your price in gold, and I shall pay it."

Dvalinn shrugged his shoulders derisively. "These caves, and those in our home Svartálfheim, provide all the gold and silver we require. You cannot acquire Brísingamen by paying for it with coin."

There was an implication in this answer, and so Freyja persevered: "How, then, can I attain this wondrous necklace?"

The dark elf responded with a leer: "We have poured all our art, all our magical skill, into making Brísingamen. You would need to lie with me, and with my three assistants, for it to be a fair recompense for our efforts. Then we would let you have it."

Freyja was powerful; she could wrench the necklace from the hands of the elf, or strike all four of them dead and walk away with the jewel. But she was worshipped as the mother of all creatures, the goddess of love. Such deeds, she felt, were not permissible.

However, she was irritated by the audacity of these

creatures that demanded to buy her favors. "What makes you think I would agree to such a debased transaction?" she asked, in an icy tone.

Dvalinn lowered his head in a sign of contrition. "I only asked because your beauty surpasses anything I have experienced in my humble life. I would do anything to have you in my arms, and all I can offer is this necklace into which I have poured all my being. It seems fair to give you eternal enjoyment of an object as precious as Brísingamen at the cost of only a few minutes of your time and attention." The dark elf pointed to the storm that raged outside the entrance of the cave above them. "You have no place to go right now. Why don't you spend the next few hours with us?"

While they talked, the other elves had been applying final touches to the necklace; one ping here, a scraping there. Finally, Alfrik declared: "It's finished!" The remaining two elves, Berling and Grer, chimed in: "It's done!" and "It's perfect!" They held the necklace close to the furnace and the just-completed Brísingamen transformed the dimness of the chamber into midday splendor.

Dvalinn's upturned face reflected his desire. "See, my Lady," he argued, "the necklace is ready for you to wear. It cannot enhance your beauty, but will complement it!"

For the first time, Freyja regarded the dark elf with some interest. Like others of his kind, Dvalinn was short-legged and stocky, with dark skin that seemed to absorb the light from the cave's burning fires. His arms were disproportionately long and powerful, perhaps the fruit of decades of bending metals to his will; the hands were large, with strong and precise fingers. Freyja could only see part of the elf's face, for the top was covered with a woolen cap and the lower half was shrouded by an abundant beard. Only Dvalinn's eyes were clearly visible, and shone with a radiance that evidenced intelligence, willfulness, and greed. Obviously, a creature not to be ignored. Like the other gods of Ásgard, Freyja felt disdain towards dark elves, but this one demanded her full consideration.

Freyja weighed in her mind the cost in revulsion and shame against the benefit of being the sole possessor of an object of unsurpassed beauty. Her vanity won over—this day's debasement would vanish before long, but the joy and pride she would experience by owning and displaying Brísingamen would remain hers forever. Her decision took only a few seconds.

"Fine," she relented. "Do you have a chamber where we can retire?"

Dvalinn pointed wordlessly to a dark opening behind the workshop.

"Who goes first?" she asked coldly, not looking forward to what would soon ensue.

"I am their leader. I will do the honors first."

By the time Freyja emerged from the back chamber, the storm had run its course. The feeble light of a winter afternoon sun shone from the cave entrance, where the cats waited, pacing impatiently against the return of their mistress. Freyja was wearing Brísingamen around her neck. She noticed for the first time, with a pleasure that she hoped would be repeated over and over through the years, how the pallid sun's rays were amplified into a cascade of light emanating from her breast. Turning skyward, Freyja engaged in a bit of bragging: "Sól, you are a woman like I, but when I wear this necklace, I surpass you in splendor."

The sun did not respond, but Freyja smiled in anticipation of the envious looks that all females, whatever their nature and status, would cast on the inimitable object she now owned. There had been a lot of pain, discomfort, and humiliation involved in obtaining it, but Brísingamen was worth the cost.

Several months after acquiring the priceless necklace, Freya and her consort Odin were guests at a banquet held by Ægir, the sea god. It was a large gathering, attended by most of the important gods residing in Ásgard. Among the guests was Loki, the malicious shape-shifter, whose presence was only tolerated by the others because of his blood brother kinship with Odin. Also in attendance were Bragi, Odin's son and god of poetry, with his wife Idunn; Tyr, the god of war; Njord, the god of the wind, and Skadi his wife; Freyr, brother of Freyja; Vithar, son of Odin; and many other gods, elves, and other beings.

Large kettles of ale had been provided for the feast and consumed little by little and, as was common on those occasions, the guests became increasingly inebriated as the night progressed. At length, the company engaged in a round of *flyting*, a contest in which parties flung insults at each other in verse. Loki, who had come uninvited to the feast, soon was trading acid barbs with most of the gods and goddesses in attendance. At one point, Loki leveled a charge of promiscuity against the goddess Frigg, a soothsayer who knew and, if she so chose, could manipulate the fates of gods and humans. Freyja rose to defend Frigg and told Loki that he was insane for defaming Frigg, who knew the fate of everyone and could denounce him if she wished. Loki responded with a sneer:

"You, Freyja, best remain silent for I know all about you! For you are not lacking in shame, and the gold necklace that you wear around your neck was purchased not long ago by selling yourself to not one, or two, or three, but *four* svartálfar."

Freyja paled, and then vigorously objected to the accusation. "You lie, Loki. You raise false allegations about the misdeeds of others, for you know that everyone present is furious at you and you want to have your revenge in anticipation of being expelled."

Njord rose to defend his daughter Freyja and declared: "A woman enjoying the amorous company of a lover in addition to that of her husband is not unusual or harmful, and you, Loki, should know, for you have been a woman to many males and have even borne their offspring. You are base and a pervert!"

In the normal course of a *flyting* contest, matters would have subsided or insults shifted in another direction, but Loki retorted with unfeigned seriousness: "I do not jest. I learned of Freyja's *transaction* with the dark elves from one of the participants. In claiming to be innocent, Freyja has perjured herself!"

Odin had remained silent up to that moment, for he and Loki were sworn brothers. He tolerated most of Loki's misdeeds, but he could not let the accusation of harlotry against Freyja remain unrebutted. He rose and said in a steady but threatening voice:

"Loki, if true, your words would cast a pall of shame on

the reputation of my consort. Either state the facts that support your accusation or withdraw it and apologize to her. You had a lot to drink and exceeded the bounds of *flyting*, so I am inclined to be forgiving, but by insulting Freyja you offend me as well."

Loki blanched, for he was familiar with Odin's spear Gungnir, whose carved runes ensured its aim and would bring death to whoever became Odin's target. He replied placatingly: "Would that my words were only harmless banter, cast out as part of a convivial pastime. But that is not the case. Let me tell you how I know."

Loki adopted a dramatic pose and continued, "A few nights ago, I followed my usual practice of traveling around Ásgard in disguise to learn what deeds, just and foul, were being carried out by its inhabitants. During my journey, I came across a deep cave that I had not noticed before, and was drawn in by overhearing an animated conversation being carried on by two svartálfar as they worked. My curiosity being aroused, I entered undetected and added my essence to the existing flames of a fire pit. The two dark elves, whose names I never learned, were discussing in lurid detail a prolonged, debased sexual encounter in which they and two others of their kind had taken part. From the conversation I found out that a beautiful female goddess had exchanged her favors for a golden necklace to which the svartálfar had applied all their collective skills. They did not name the goddess, but they repeatedly identified their leader, a svartálfr named Dvalinn. It was he, the other dark elves said, who had orchestrated the encounter and had taken the lead in their perverse copulation with the goddess. Based on the description of the female and the necklace, I have no doubt that it was Freyja they were talking about, and the necklace no other than that Brísingamen, the singular object she is wearing around her neck even now."

Odin was not about to be easily convinced of his consort's culpability. "That is too much guessing on your part to support such a lurid tale. Plus, those base creatures are known to be cunning and may not be telling the truth, even to each other." He shook his head, reflected on Loki's claims, and came to a decision. "Loki, your tracking skills are second to no one's. Go underground to Svartálfheim and search through its endless tunnels and caverns until you find a dark elf by the name of Dvalinn. Bring him to me at Valhalla. I shall get to the bottom of this. Someone is bound to taste Gungnir's blade yet."

Loki was gone for a long time. When at last he returned, he proceeded directly to Valhalla, carrying a closed sack whose contents heaved mightily in a futile attempt to escape.

It was dinner-time and the great hall of the palace was teeming with hundreds of dead heroes, the einherjar, who after a day of fighting with each other had recovered from their wounds and were feasting with meat from the giant boar Saehrimnir and mead from the udder of the goat Heidrun. Odin presided, sitting sullenly on his throne, eating nothing but feeding pieces of meat to his wolves.

Odin's expression became one of interest as his blood brother approached his throne. "What have you there, brother?" he asked eagerly.

"A rather rambunctious svartálfr, freshly captured." He was about to open the sack when a gesture from Odin brought his motion to a halt.

"Not here. This matter must be handled among us, in private. Let us go to my quarters." Summoning one of the valkyrjur serving at the banquet, he instructed her: "Please find my consort Freyja; she is somewhere in Valhalla. Bring her to my quarters right away." The maiden left, quick as lightning, and Odin led Loki and his sack through several rooms before reaching the huge chamber that served as his working and sleeping quarters. Odin went up a dais and sat on his royal chair, waiting impatiently, arms crossed before his chest, a broadsword resting between his knees.

Before long, the valkyrja returned, escorting a surprised Freyja who held still in her hand a set of pruning shears. "My Lord, I was outdoors, trimming and shaping the lower branches of Glasir to make your favorite tree look even more beautiful. What is your pleasure?"

"We may soon have some pruning of our own to do," replied Odin harshly. Then, to Loki: "You may proceed."

Loki opened the sack and extracted a writhing figure, who he held by the neck with an iron grip. "This scoundrel is Dvalinn, the svartálfr. I had a hard time finding him, and an even harder one persuading him to enter this sack!"

"What do you want with me?" bellowed the dark elf defiantly. "I owe no fealty to you, but to my fellow svartál-far. I don't belong in Ásgard, and demand that you let me go!"

"Yet not long ago, you were spending some time in a cave along the road in Ásgard, is that not so?" questioned Loki, assuming the role of prosecutor.

"That was a special case. The walls of that cave hold small amounts of a very rare red gemstone I needed to adorn a neckband I was fashioning." The moment Dvalinn uttered this explanation, his eyes focused on a tall woman standing next to the chair of the seated lord. He took a deep breath and fell silent.

"That neckband you were fashioning, did it look like the necklace now worn by the lady that stands across the room from you?" accused Loki.

Dvalinn started trembling and said nothing. At length, the seated man spoke for the first time. He cautioned: "Answer the question truthfully, svartálfr, for your life may be at stake here."

Dvalinn gulped, incapable of thinking out a way to dissemble. "Yes, it looks something like that."

Loki retorted without a pause: "In fact, the neckband you were fashioning *was* the necklace that is now being worn by this lady, a famous adornment that you named Brísingamen, is that not right?"

"It could be . . ." replied Dvalinn, feeling trapped.

"Do you consider Brísingamen to be a well-crafted piece of jewelry?"

Dvalinn's face filled with pride. "It is one of my greatest masterpieces. Built with all my craft, infused with all my magic."

"How did Brísingamen come to be in the lady's possession?"

"I gave it to her," was the despairing answer.

"How much coin did she give for it?"

A deep silence enveloped the room. Then, in a reluctant whisper, Dvalinn answered: "None."

"What prompted such a generous act on your part?" drilled Loki, implacable.

Dvalinn felt like a cornered animal, confronting the inexorable threat that faced him. He stared ahead in panic.

The seated lord appeared to be holding his breath, anger written on his face. The lady standing next to him seemed to have shrunken, folded into herself, arms crossed against her bosom, face contorted in sorrow and shame. She started to speak, but the sounds that left her lips were incoherent.

Only Dvalinn's captor was enjoying the moment, glancing at him with glee, ready for the inevitable answer.

Would he lie? Could he deny the crowning moment of his long existence, betray the infinite pleasure he had experienced holding Freyja in his arms? His life passed before his eyes, and everything he had done before and after his encounter with the goddess seemed like dust, inconsequential trivia compared with the boundless joy of that coupling. He could not disown it. The words came out one by one, like heavy stones, dropping into the air.

"I asked her to lie with me as payment for the necklace."

"And did she agree?"

Odin rose from his chair as if bitten by a viper, and charged towards the elf, broadsword in hand. Dvalinn cowered and, as Odin raised the weapon in preparation to strike, he uttered the final, fatal answer:

"Yes, she did. And those were the most enjoyable moments of my life . . ."

The rest of Dvalinn's reply, if there was to be one, was silenced by the sword blow that severed his head.

As the headless corpse of the elf fell to the ground, an image was engraved into his no-longer-seeing eyes: A woman, trembling with embarrassment and pity, clasping a great necklace whose every stone had turned the color of blood.

Heimdall and Loki

O'er the sea from the north | there sails a ship
With the people of Hel, | at the helm stands Loki
Völuspá, Stanza 51

ALL THE STONES SET IN THE GOLDEN NECKLACE known as Brísingamen had turned blood red upon the beheading of Dvalinn, the black elf who had led the crafting of the incomparable jewel. Thus transformed, the necklace became a perennial badge of shame, fingering goddess Freyja as an adulteress who had traded her favors for possession of the necklace.

Freyja, however, continued to wear Brísingamen. Perhaps it was vanity, or wounded pride, or indifference to the opinions of others. Whatever the reason, she kept the necklace glittering in all its glory as the light of the sun shone on it, eliciting gasps of admiration and scorn from gods and humans alike.

Only one being failed to be awed by Freyja's display. Odin, the Allfather, felt rage fill his chest every time he saw the necklace and was reminded of his wife's infidelity. Often, he was tempted to order Freyja to take Brísingamen off, or forcibly remove the necklace from her neck. Only prudence restrained him from taking action against his wayward wife. For the head of the gods knew that resorting to violence would cause an eternal rift between him and Freyja, which he dared not unleash. Thus, Odin resorted to stealth to remove the odious object from public display. He summoned his blood brother Loki for a secret conversation.

"Loki, how are your thieving skills these days?"

"Never better," replied the trickster god with an inquisitive tilting of the head. "Why do you ask?"

"I may want you to apply your skills to solve a little problem I am having."

"What is the problem?"

"One that you created in part. At Ægir's banquet you exposed that my consort Freyja had procured Brísingamen by sleeping with several dark elves, causing me great shame and the need to put to death the leader of those svartálfar."

"Yes, I remember the affair rather well. Indeed, I was able to find the main culprit and bring him before you, and got him to confess his crime before you lopped off his head," boasted Loki.

"Exactly. The problem is that Freyja insists on wearing Brísingamen, reminding everyone that she made a cuckold out of me. I want that necklace to disappear!"

"And you want me to . . ."

"Yes, steal it from her. I don't care how you do it or what you do with the necklace. You can destroy it or sell it to whoever you want."

"And you will defend me if the truth comes out?"

"Of course. I always have."

"Well, it will be a challenge. Let me think about it."

Loki approached the sleeping Freyja in the form of a miniscule gnat. Though virtually invisible, he knew that the slightest touch against Freyja's skin would give him away. Therefore, the only way he could safely remove

Brísingamen would be to unfasten its gold clasp and catch the necklace as it tumbled to the ground. But tampering with the mechanism risked brushing against the goddess. After much deliberation, he emitted a tiny flame from one of the gnat's legs and applied it to the clasp, aiming to melt it down.

It was a slow, laborious task, and extended for several hours. He had to stop and fly away a few times as Freyja tossed and turned, threatening to wake up. But she remained asleep, and after every interruption Loki returned patiently to his task.

It was almost dawn by the time the melting clasp thinned itself enough to break and unlatch the necklace. Loki waited expectantly as Freyja's sleeping motions caused Brísingamen to slip off her neck and slide towards the ground. Metamorphosing into a falcon, Loki snatched the necklace with his beak and flew away in triumph.

The moment Freyja opened her eyes she realized something was wrong. Her neck felt light, as if a heavy weight had been removed from it. She raised a hand to her throat in search of the pleasant feel of her necklace, and the hand touched her flesh without an intervening obstacle. She panicked. "Brísingamen has been stolen!!!" Freyja's screams resonated throughout Ásgard.

Odin was among the first to react to his consort's desperate cries. Assuming a concerned air while secretly laughing inside, he rode to Sessrúmnir, Freyja's palace, and demanded: "What is the matter, my dear? Has a bad dream troubled your sleep?"

"It's no dream!! Someone has snatched Brísingamen while I slept!"

"Who could possibly have done that?" he replied, feigning innocence.

"There is only one being evil enough to attempt such a deed and skillful enough to carry it out: your blood brother Loki!"

"Now, let us not jump to hasty conclusions. I will personally interrogate Loki and try to get to the bottom of this!"

But Loki had disappeared from Ásgard and all efforts

to find him proved fruitless. Odin even sent his ravens, Huginn and Muninn, to roam across Ásgard, and then through Midgard and all the other realms, in search for the god. He could not be found.

Finally, Odin felt forced to summon his son Heimdall. "You have the sharpest eyes, the keenest ears, the most sensitive nose, of all the gods. Find where Loki is hiding and bring him to face judgment before me."

Heimdall, who had no affection for Loki, smiled at the assignment, despite its difficulty. "With pleasure, father!"

There was no exaggeration in Odin's praise for Heimdall's skills. Father and son had once gone together to the world tree Yggdrasil and each made a sacrifice to Mimir, the guardian of the well under the tree, in a quest to enhance their powers. Odin gave up an eye to achieve wisdom and mystical sight, while Heimdall sacrificed an ear to enhance his senses. As a result, Heimdall could see at night just as well as if it were day, and for over a hundred leagues; his hearing was so keen that he could hear grass as it grew on the earth; his sense of smell so well developed he could perceive the fragrance of the roses that bloomed in the human gardens in Midgard.

Heimdall unsuccessfully traversed most of the routes others had followed in search of elusive Loki, and then went beyond others' efforts. Aided by his supernatural senses, he combed through high mountains and deep valleys, then plunged into the vast ocean that surrounds Midgard, where dwells Jörmungandr, the Midgard Serpent.

Heimdall skirted the lair of the serpent and combed the ocean from one end to the other. He was about to give up when, from the very depths of the waters, he detected a faint aroma: a complex smell of sun-warmed woods, hay, leather, and woodsmoke. Heimdall knew that unique smell very well, and it betrayed his target.

He plummeted, descending into the consuming darkness for a very long time. When he reached the sandy bottom, he became aware of a rocky cavern with an entrance hidden by marine growth. Loki's smell emanated from that cavern.

"Loki, come out! I know you are there!" challenged

Heimdall. There was no answer. But suddenly, a large shark emerged, heading towards him with malicious intent. Heimdall transformed himself into a giant octopus and mounted the shark in an embrace that threatened to crush it. They struggled; the shark attempted mightily to bite his foe, but Heimdall tightened his hold until Loki's breathing became labored. He gasped and uttered feebly: "I yield. Please release me!"

"Not until you hand over Freyja's necklace!"

"I don't have it!" protested Loki.

"You lie!" countered Heimdall. "I can see the jewel's glow inside your belly! Give it up!"

There was a gurgling sound, and the shark's mouth erupted with the release of Brísingamen. The necklace began to drop towards the ocean floor, but Heimdall retrieved it quickly with a tentacle.

"I should dispatch you to your daughter Hel's domain," threatened Heimdall. "But you are my father's blood brother, so I will take you to him. He can decide on your punishment."

Heimdall rose to the surface and turned himself into an

eagle, carrying Loki in his talons as if he were a tiny fish. Loki fought with all his might to free himself, but Heimdall was second only to Thor in strength and so kept Loki firmly in his grip. Writhing with anger and shame, Loki issued a threat: "I shall have my revenge for this, Heimdall! Mark my words!"

Odin, himself a guilty party, let Loki off with a stern rebuke and delivered Brísingamen back to Freyja, who never let go of the necklace again and continued to wear it to her consort's silent abashment. Odin, however, needed to reward Heimdall for his gallant deed.

"You have proved yourself a most skilled warrior, a worthy protector of the gods. I shall build you a great dwelling where the rainbow bridge Bifröst marks the entrance to Ásgard. There you shall stand guard against any and all enemies who may threaten us."

Thus, for ages to follow, Heimdall watched and listened for the approach of the gods' enemies. He had been furnished with a gigantic horn, Gjallarhorn, which he would blow to alert all nine realms of the universe to the impending approach of invaders bent on the overthrow of the Æsir. According to predictions, this would occur during Ragnarøkkr, the end of the world.

After centuries of unwavering watch, at last his keen senses perceived the approach of two armies. One by sea led by Loki, while the other came by land, headed by the immense fire giant Surtr. The fire giants approached trampling on the rainbow bridge, marching into Ásgard. Soon the final battle between the gods and their enemies was fought. Among the encounters that took place that fateful day, Heimdall squared off against Loki.

As the adversaries approached each other, Heimdall raised his enchanted sword Höfud, so keen that it could pierce the essence of a god, intending to cut Loki in half. However, he failed in his attempt, for Loki became an invisible burst of wind from which emerged a flaming shaft aimed at Heimdall's heart.

Both gods engaged time and again, Heimdall unable to see anything of his adversary except for Loki's spear of flame, with which he parried Höfud. But suddenly, the wind storm that was Loki let out a small burst of his fragrance. Heimdall followed its origin with a wild thrust of Höfud. The sword found its target, but in launching his charge Heimdall had left himself open to a piercing stab by Loki's flaming spear, which ran him through.

Both gods fell to the ground simultaneously. Loki, no longer invisible, exhibited a savage slash that ran from neck to groin, bleeding profusely. The fiery lance that had impaled Heimdall protruded from his chest, which was charred by an all-consuming fire.

Heimdall went to his death silently. Loki, however, had time to issue three hateful words: "Revenge is mine!" He was dead as he uttered them.

Odin's Other Eye

*Then arises Hlín's second grief, when Odin goes with the wolf to fight,
and the bright slayer of Beli with Surt. Then will Frigg's beloved fall.*
Völuspá, Stanza 53

THE CLIFFS BROKE OPEN and fire giants from Muspelheim swarmed into Midgard, led by a chieftain named Surtr who brandished a flaming sword brighter than the sun. They marched across the rainbow bridge to Ásgard, advancing towards Valhalla, the fortress of the gods. Their stomping feet broke the bridge, which fell into the void amidst a deafening crash.

When the rainbow bridge collapsed, Heimdall the sentinel raised the Gjallarhorn into the air and blew it forcefully, issuing an ominous blast that heralded the beginning of the end of the gods.

Alerted to the impending peril, Odin rode to the world tree Yggdrasill and approached the well at the tree's roots.

There he met the embalmed head of Mimir, the dead sage who knows all that is, all that has been, and all that may in the future occur.

"I come to you, O great Mimir, as I did once before, to obtain wisdom in this direst of all hours."

"What ill news brings you here?"

"Ragnarøkkr is upon us!"

"Have there been portents of its coming?"

"There has been a Great Winter lasting for three years with no mitigating summers in between. The wolves Skoll and Hati, who have hunted the sun and the moon through the skies since the beginning of time, have caught their prey and darkened the heavens. Jörmungandr, the serpent encircling the world, has released its tail from its mouth, flooding the seas, and has thrashed onto the land, spraying poison to fill the air and water. The ship Naglfar has left its moorings, and carries an army of frost giants led by Loki, freed from his chains. Finally, the great wolf Fenrisúlfr, whom I reared myself, runs across the earth with fire blazing from his eyes and nostrils, devouring everything in his path."

"And what is your question?"

"What can we do to prevail against the forces of evil now that Ragnarøkkr has arrived?"

"You once gave up an eye to be allowed to drink from this well and gain wisdom. What do you have to offer this time?"

"My other eye?"

"You would be useless, and would be lucky if your steed Sleipnir could carry you safely back to Valhalla. What else do you have to offer?"

"Only my life."

"Sacrificing your life will gain you nothing. The dead cannot put their wisdom to use."

"I have nothing else to trade. We are all doomed!"

"Nay. I can tell you for free what you may do to prevent the world's destruction in the upcoming final battle. But the cost to you of averting such doom will be dearer than losing your life."

"How can that possibly be?"

"Dying, however painful, is over at some point. What would await you is eternal agony, without surcease."

"You speak in riddles. Pray tell me plainly what I must do."

"You shall meet Fenrisúlfr in battle upon the field called Vigrid. There, you and the wolf shall face off in mortal combat. The wolf will kill you and be slain. At the same time, encounters between the Æsir and the forces of Loki will rage all over the battlefield, resulting in everyone's annihilation. Everything, good and evil, will be destroyed, and Ragnarøkkr will run to its bitter end. Unless . . ."

"Unless what?"

"Unless you flee the battlefield. Your flight will break the spirits of your subjects and allow Loki and his cohorts to prevail. The evil ones, once victorious, will permit those who survive the battle to continue to exist, now in thrall to them."

"And what will happen to me?"

"Loki will spare you, but he will have you chained for all eternity. He will also put out your other eye, rendering you blind forever."

"You must be jesting to propose such an outcome."

"I speak in earnest, for even after death I would mourn

for the end of all that exists. That is the only way to avoid the ultimate calamity."

"The choices you present to me are equally unacceptable."

"Nonetheless, you must choose one outcome or the other, and do so very soon."

Upon his return to Valhalla, Odin brushed aside the questions about his meeting with the head of Mimir, for he did not want the other gods to become discouraged. After a brief counsel, they all donned their armor and rushed to Vigrid to do battle with the fire giants and other monsters, who were already arriving.

Odin rode on Sleipnir wielding Gungnir, the magical spear that never missed its target. At the head of the enemy armies, he spotted his blood brother Loki and threw Gungnir at him, intending to bring his existence to an end. But Loki turned himself into a tiny glowing cinder; the spear flew over him and struck one of the fire giants, embedding itself in its corpse. Unable to dislodge Gungnir,

Odin was left without his favored weapon as the battle continued.

Soon Loki's spawn, the wolf and the serpent, arrived and brought chaos as they inundated Vigrid, filling it with debris. Odin faced Fenrisúlfr, his stern gaze meeting the fiery eyes of the beast. "Ho, Fenrisúlfr, must we test each other in battle? Do you not recall that I was the one who allowed you to remain in Ásgard and raised you as my own kin?"

The wolf's fiery eyes gleamed with hate as it snarled its response: "You also snared me and kept me in captivity for millennia until I escaped my chains. I owe you nothing. And know that wolf cubs are apt to turn on their forebearers."

As Fenrisúlfr advanced towards him, Odin made a gesture that summoned the vast army of the Einherjar, the dead heroes he had kept in Valhalla to assist him in the final battle. The human army attacked the wolf from all directions, attempting to pierce its massive body with their swords and lances. To no avail; the hide of Fenrisúlfr was hard as iron and deflected all blows. Then the wolf opened its gigantic jaws and started to devour the warriors as if they were nibbles, until they were all consumed.

"Thanks for the tidbits you provided!" growled the wolf as it faced Odin again. "Now for the main course. Come to me!" Fenrisúlfr's maw opened so wide that its upper jaw touched the heavens, and the wolf advanced upon its adversary.

Could such an exalted deity as Odin ever have experienced fear? No one knows. But an icy chill coursed through the Æsir's spine as he drew his broadsword and steeled himself to meet his enemy. As he did, the words of Mimir resounded in his ears: "Retreat, and you shall live, and the world shall not perish!"

Odin pulled at the reins of Sleipnir as if to make his steed turn away from the approaching wolf. Noticing his gesture, Fenrisúlfr let out a brutal laugh that shook the earth's every stone: "Run, you fool! I will catch you wherever you go!" And then, addressing Sleipnir, it added: "And you, little brother, throw your rider! I will be generous and let you live, but he must perish!"

Sleipnir, enraged at the wolf's words, turned around.

Disregarding the pull of Odin's reins, he galloped towards Fenrisúlfr's open mouth and in two strides had plunged into it. Fenrisúlfr closed its jaws around horse and rider.

Only the Norns know whether Odin regained courage from the valor of his steed, or if he decided that extinction of the world's inhabitants was preferable to their survival in servitude to evil. Be that as it may, Odin thrust his broadsword into the roof of Fenrisúlfr's mouth, intending to force it open so he could ride in and strike at the beast's heart. Alas, the sword's blows were mere insect bites to the monster. The wolf spit out the sword and started to gulp, seeking to swallow the god and his mount.

Odin resorted to the only weapon still left to him. In a gesture that mimicked another he had made a long time before, he gouged his left eye from its socket and cast it into the wolf's throat, voicing an incantation that summoned all his power. The eye became a ball of fire that grew in size and intensity as it erupted in the wolf's throat and filled the mouth's cavity, incinerating Odin and Sleipnir, and consuming the inside of Fenrisúlfr's head.

The wolf writhed in mortal agony, the banging of its

massive body cracking the surface of the earth, causing an earthquake that scattered asunder the bodies of gods and monsters, live and slain, that dotted the scene of universal carnage that Vigrid had become.

An utter silence, more daunting than the din of battle that had preceded it, filled the ravaged earth. Nothing moved save for two crows, Odin's witnesses, who would course the skies seeking in vain a living being to whom they could relate what had come to pass that fatal day.

Baldr's Return

All ills grow better, and Baldr comes back;
Baldr and Hoth dwell in Hropt's battle-hall
Völuspá, Stanza 62

THE WEDDING OF ODIN'S SON BALDR to the human princess Nanna was an extravagant affair in which all the Æsir took part. So did delegations from all the inhabited worlds: Gullweig came, representing the Æsir-friendly gods from Vanaheim; Hrungnir came, on behalf of the frost giants of Jötunheim; light elves came from Álfheim and dark ones from Svartálfheim; even humans from Midgard were invited. They all attended, not only out of respect for Odin, but because his son was almost universally loved and appreciated. Baldr was fair and bright, well-spoken and gracious, strong and nimble, and wisest among the gods, such that no one could find fault with his judgments.

One not joining in Baldr's acclaim was his brother

Höder, who was incensed by Nanna's choosing Baldr over him when both brothers had courted her. For that reason, Höder spent the celebration leaning against an ash tree, sulking and mumbling imprecations at the wedding couple as the rest of the party enjoyed the festivities.

Behind the ash tree stood Loki, the god of mischief, who took pleasure in causing grief to others. Loki heard Höder's tirade and commented: "It is for females to complain about their fate, and do nothing about it. True males act to right the wrongs that have been done to them."

Höder reacted angrily to Loki's berating and turned as if to strike him, but stopped short at Loki's next words: "You are a brave Æsir, so you must seek some retribution for the ill your brother has inflicted on you. I will be happy to assist you in that endeavor, if you will allow me."

Höder was simple-minded and did not capture the depth of treachery underlying Loki's words. He replied dubiously: "Yes, retribution would be nice. Should I try striking him now?"

"No, not now," replied Loki. "If you attack him before this big crowd, they will separate the two of you the moment the fight starts. It must be done later, at a time and in a manner such that nobody can interfere. Also, I need time to think of how I can assist you. For the moment, let Baldr have his day of joy. Go stag hunting and cool off. I will come to you when I'm ready."

Disguised as an old farmer, Loki traveled to the mountains that ringed Ásgard's Plain of Idavöll. There, in virtually inaccessible hillside crags, dwelled the völva, the staff-bearing seeresses who were masters of the arcane arts.

Loki was looking for one Thorbjorg, a völva famed for her skills in *seidr*, the potent Norse magic. He found Thorbjorg in her dwelling, a cottage high on a hill overlooking Baldr's magnificent palace Breidablik. Loki asserted that he needed help to get rid of a large bear that was decimating his cattle and asked the völva to prepare the most toxic liquid poison her art could conjure.

Thorbjorg was adept at divination and, recognizing Loki, understood his true intent and was sympathetic to his aim. The constant sight of Baldr's power and magnificence rankled her mean spirit. "I can brew a potion from berries and leaves of the mistletoe, together with certain other ingredients. If taken internally it can kill a Jötunn in three heartbeats. Would that suffice?"

Loki was dubious. "Can you make it extra strong?"

Thorbjorg smiled evilly. "You must be beset by a particularly large bear. But yes, I shall."

Loki returned to Höder months later, and handed the god a jar containing a greenish paste. "Apply this unguent to your weapons and it will make them twice as swift. But be careful not to let it enter your body in any manner, for it is very potent."

Loki's reappearance came as the gods were about to gather again for a feast on the birth of Baldr's son Forseti. Odin had announced that this feast would include a contest in which attendees would take turns flinging spears and shooting arrows at Baldr, who was renowned for his agility and the thickness of his skin. "Anyone who can hit Baldr and draw even a drop of blood from him will win a magic golden cup that never runs empty," announced the sovereign.

One after another, the gods, giants and elves in attendance attempted to strike Baldr with their projectiles. Baldr jumped, slid, dove, and twisted, placing himself just out of reach of each incoming missile. Even Thor, egged on by Odin, tossed his magic hammer Mjölnir gently at his brother. There was no way Baldr could avoid a hammer that never missed its target, but Mjölnir struck the god in the chest and caromed away, as Baldr's skin was hard as iron and absorbed the blow harmlessly.

Höder was one of the last contestants. He brandished a javelin, a light, narrow spear that glistened oddly in the afternoon sun. Nobody paid much attention to him—they never did. He planted himself across from his brother and threw the javelin at Baldr with all his might, but poor aim.

Loki, who had turned himself into an almost invisible speck of dust, climbed upon the javelin and directed it at Baldr, who was smiling at his brother's errant throw until the javelin corrected itself. At the last moment, it struck Baldr squarely in the chest. Loki, who was still controlling the weapon, thrust it into Baldr, forcing his skin to yield to the javelin's metal tip. It drew a stream of blood as the spear traversed Baldr's body.

Loki swiftly fled as all eyes focused on Baldr, who staggered forward a few steps, fell to the ground shaking violently, and drew still.

Höder ran to his brother, lying immobile on the ground. "O, Brother, wake up! I only meant to tickle you, not injure you!" But Baldr would not respond to anyone in this world, god or mortal, ever again.

Odin ordered that his fallen son be given a fitting funeral. Baldr's corpse was laid within his ship, Hringhorni. The vessel was turned into a gigantic funeral pyre and launched into the sea, after Odin paid his respects in an emotional farewell. Baldr's widow, Nanna, was overcome with grief and died as Hringhorni was being launched. Her corpse was also fed to the pyre.

Baldr's *hamingja*, the part of his being that embodied his better qualities, abandoned his corpse and descended to

Niflheim to become a thrall of Hel, the goddess of the dead. Not long thereafter, Baldr was joined in Hel by his brother Höder, freshly dead under circumstances that were never fully discerned. It was said that he had been slain by Váli, a son sired by Odin to avenge the death of Baldr.

Following Baldr's funeral, it was revealed that Loki had played a part in Baldr's slaying. Höder confessed that Loki had instructed him to fling the javelin at Baldr, and had supplied the mistletoe coating that delivered the deadly poison into Baldr's body. Loki was reviled for such an evil deed, and the hatred the other gods felt against him only multiplied when he bragged about having played a leading role in the tragedy. Eventually, Loki was captured and imprisoned in a cavern, where he remained until breaking loose on Ragnarøkkr, the day the world ended.

The fires that destroyed all the world during Ragnarøkkr reached Niflheim and laid waste to Hel's domain. The goddess, who was Loki's daughter and drew her essence from him, perished when her father was slain by

Heimdall, and the *hamingjas* of her captives were released. Among those freed after Hel's demise were Baldr's and Höder's *hamingjas*.

The world that was destroyed on Ragnarøkkr had been created by Odin and his brothers Vili and Ve. Upon that world's demise and Odin's death, his surviving brothers took it upon themselves to create a new world, free of the imperfections that had plagued the old one. Finally, a beautiful reborn world arose from the ashes of death and destruction. The *hamingjas* of Baldr and Hödr rose to the new world and implanted themselves in the spirits of children who had just been conceived by Ragnarøkkr's surviving humans, Líf and Lífthrasir, from who came so numerous an offspring that the new world was fully repeopled.

Baldr thus will live again in a new world where the earth sprouts abundance without the need of sowing seed. Baldr will grow to rule the renewed world in peace and justice, and from time to time the reconciled brothers will join the surviving Æsir, Vídarr and Váli and the sons of Thor, Módi and Magni. Then all shall sit down together and hold speech with one another upon the plain of Idavöll, the meeting place of the gods. Together, they all shall call to mind their secret wisdom, and speak of those events which happened before, in an earlier time in another world, and rejoice in the blessings of the renewed one.

END

About the Author

Matias Travieso-Diaz is a former engineer and attorney who, following retirement, redirected his efforts towards fiction writing. He lives with his daughter and two dogs in the Washington, D.C. area. He describes himself as an "*Animal Farm* goat, Packers and Barça fan, and lover of opera, classical theater, jazz, Italian food and vino." He is the author of numerous short stories, and two novels: *The Taíno Women*, set in Cuba's early colonial period, and *The Travels of Lázaro Serrano*, set in Cuba and Jamaica in 1762–63. *The Satchel and other Terrors*, a collection of some of his published short stories, was released in February 2023 and is available through Amazon and other retailers. Additional collections of his stories are scheduled for publication in 2025.

About Pink Hydra Press

Founded in 2024 to make a space for new, queer, and weird speculative literature, Pink Hydra Press is the only organization of its kind in Africa. The genre/lit magazine The Pink Hydra has published short stories and poems from dozens of international authors. The book press is just starting out.

If you enjoy stories with a touch of the weird, or if you're an author who loves writing books and poetry infused with weirdness, come visit us at www.thepinkhydra.com.

We publish a variety of genres, but we are particularly interested in queer science fiction and fantasy, stories written by and about women, stories which challenge the current status quo, and spicy romantic and erotic stories.

Many heads. One mission.